Tacenda Literary Magazine

2016 Edition

Editor-In-Chief
Marisa Fein

Consulting Editor
Robert Johnson

Cover Design
Carla Mavaddat

Text Design
Sonia Tabriz

BleakHouse Publishing
2016

Ward Circle Building 254
American University
Washington, DC 20016

NEC Box 67
New England College
Henniker, New Hampshire 03242
www.BleakHousePublishing.com

Robert Johnson – Editor & Publisher
Sonia Tabriz - Managing Editor
Liz Calka - Creative Director

Casey Chiappetta – Chief Operating Officer
Alexa Marie Kelly – Chief Editorial Officer
Emily Dalgo – Chief Development Officer
Rachel Ternes – Chief Creative Officer

Carla Mavaddat – Art Director
Ella Decker – Art Curator

ISBN: 978-0-9961162-2-0

Printed in the United States of America

A Note From the Editor

TACENDA: n., pronounced ta'KEN'da
'things better left unsaid'

At BleakHouse Publishing, we know that life continues behind bars, that humanity endures within the confines of a prison cell.

The following collection aims to put a finger to the pulse of the criminal justice system. Each poem or short story highlights the systematic injustices and prejudices of a system that has and continues to forever change the lives of those it touches.

Whether it be a first-hand account of everyday prison life or a reflection on racial biases, every entry holds a mirror up to our culture of crime and punishment and is not afraid of its reflection.

Our work would not be possible without Professor Robert Johnson, our Consulting Editor, mentor, and unwavering supporter. Thank you for all that you do to encourage us to look passed labels and instead see humanity.

And, as always, thanks to our readers and contributors, those who have and continue to support this journey of working toward a better tomorrow.

Marisa Fein
Editor-in-Chief

TABLE OF CONTENTS

In and Out
Emily Paulsrud

In with a word
Out with a thousand
In as a man
Out as a number

Forgotten, invisible
Out, but never completely
Always a part of you remains in

Moments, dignity
Stolen by the courts
Processed by the machine

A day in court
So many lives
A man, a woman,
Pleading
Too many, silent,
Knowing too well
They might end in a cell

In and out
But not in a second
Never just a quick day in court
People processed, people waiting
Far too long,
Out of life, in the court

Slave to structure
Free of thought

Freedom Monroe
Vincent

Freedom is my wife
And without her it's tough
I could feel it in the air
That I will get another chance before my time is up
Because she wants me back
And plus I'm a visionary
She realizes all the good I've done
And the less bad I did
That's one of the reasons I married her

Inside a World
I.S.

I live inside a world full of lies and deception
Where money is an obsession
And I'm judged by my complexion
Please understand that this isn't a philosophy
But this is me expressing my feelings by thinking logically
I'm from a race that suffers from poverty
Low class black folks unfit for the American society
I live inside a world where I am guilty until proven
innocent
Modern day slavery, my place of imprisonment
Only 18 and yet my time is almost equivalent
Said to be a threat and danger to the American citizen
I live inside a world where police harass me everyday
Where I'm listed as a suspect in every case
Know that this is me speaking for every young black male
in every state
Who has been a victim to the system in every way
False convictions is what they call justice!
20 year sentences is what they call justice!
Unfair trials is what they call justice!
And I live inside a world where justice
Isn't justice when it comes to just, us

Untitled (Elephant)
D'Angelo

Have you even seen an elephant at the zoo
Locked up with so many chains it can barely move?
It must know that it's big enough to break those cuffs
But it thinks it's a failure and that's why it's stuck
They put chains on it when it was very young
And it fell on its face when it tried to run
Eventually it gave up hope
And now that it's strong enough to break free
It only mopes
I often feel the same pain
At one point I was free but I fell for the game
But I'm worse than the elephants, I have to be
Because the oppressor that put me here was me

My Window
Alfred "Spoken Truth"

It's been my view 2 the world 4 many years
The trees still there
Strong and majestic as they seem or appear 2 be
At times they look weak without their leaves
My window daydreams, be wishing 4 things never
achieved
My window nightmares, be haunting and to the point
I can't stand 2 sleep
Now my hours feel longer, I'm just trying 2 make it 2
another spring
That means goodbye winter, my days are getting warmer
I'm getting older, my physical telling signs of aging
It's the small things I pay attention 2 lying dormant
Like which way the wind blows, or how far up the sky
goes
I mean, do I have a place in space maybe?
Am I a product of the cosmos? Cuz my window world is
crazy
Wishing I had a bird's eye view
Amazing how they play with freedom
I even seen them play on the grounds of prisons
Teasing me, look how they just fly over the fences
I wonder, do they know how important they are?
(blessings)
And how cruel man is 2 trap them in their cages
When I look out my window, I see lost hope with
defeated faces
Messages of prison expressions, enduring hard times,
mentally stressing
Yea, I chipped my tooth taking a bite out of crime
But damn, you can't compare me 2 those wearing
dentures

They went way above my guidelines, for a first time felon
I never hurt a soul, but I'm still writing from a hurt soul,
looking out my prison window
Looking at another offender, "we don't call them convicts
anymore"
That's the quotes from these C.O.s
Things changed, it's like slavery revolved back like
recidivism's door
Its new name: Department of Corrections
How can u fix something that was never broken?
U can't break me, I'm bitter like cool breeze
Heart strong like concrete, u made me!
I'm the dragon in your dungeon, spitting spoken fire
constantly
I won't let you degrade me
When I look out my window, I try 2 see as far as I can
see
I know the only thing that can stop me is me
There's no limitation 2 thought
Who created that mountain? Or the air that we breathe?
What about the sun coming in from the east? Or the
depth of the seas?
As long as I got my window, I see what u see
Prison's not physical, it's a curse of mentality

Cast up into Heights of Liberation
Josef Krebs

Cast up into heights of liberation
By bleeding air from the big blimp balloon
That had arisen out of stalwart eruptions of emotion
Taking then launching him
Happiness surrendering to hard stares and encroaching
staggers of justification
As if laughter mattered in the face off with destiny newly
invented
Piling treasure on carpets woven in history
Before you woke up to
The possibilities slumbering in subconscious travel
On to where you're supposed to be
Believing in whatever could be
Despite it never having been seen
In his lifetime
Yet
There is always room
Somewhere
For change

A Normal Black Girl
Ciera Burch

"Why do you talk like that?" the kids at her summer
camp asked.

The camp was located not in the suburban white bread
neighborhood where she lived with her mother, but in the
much browner neighborhood of her grandparents' home.
Here they played jump rope with two ropes—double-
dutch, they called it—their dexterous hands twirling faster
and faster as they turned the ropes for the girl in the
middle who was little more than a flurry of movement.
She counted aloud with them as her sneaker-clad feet
pounded against the pavement.

"Like what?" the girl asked, but no one answered her.
They continued counting. Wrong, their eyes said,
different.

"Like she's white," she overheard one girl say as she
walked unseen toward the swings, the only solitary activity
on the small playground.

II

"You're not a normal black girl," Alexis said at lunch as the
girl finished eating as quickly as possible and stood,
poised to leave, her book bag hoisted onto her shoulder.

She tended to stay in the cafeteria only long enough to
scarf down a sandwich or half of one. She preferred to
spend her lunch period shelving books and flipping
through the ones she found the most interesting, typing
their titles into her phone to add to her Goodreads "to-

read" list later. It wasn't the first time Alexis had said it or something like it, but every time she somehow managed to make it sound like a compliment. Alexis's friends, who were not the girl's friends, nodded in agreement, placid smiles on their faces.

The girl was quiet. She didn't know what to say. She never did. Well, what am I? she wanted to ask. Instead, she murmured a faint goodbye and left, hands coming up to grip the straps of her book bag.

She didn't have to ask to get her answer. She was, according to them, an Oreo—black on the outside and white on the inside. At first it bothered her. She was being herself, who else did they want her to be? In time, she came to realize. Their acceptance of her—of her blackness that seemed like whiteness because it was different than the black they were used to—made her part of the us. The other black kids at school, the ones who shouted to each other in the hallway or had rap battles in the cafeteria. They were the ones from whom she was different. They were them. If pressed, she would admit that they were also part of the reason she preferred to spend her time in the library.

"You're so smart," Mr. Reynolds commented in her next period as he handed back papers before class. An A- marked the right hand corner of her paper in red. It was one of her favorites—her American history class. He said it as if he were surprised. And yet he avoided looking at her whenever black people popped up in their class discussions, which happened often considering the class followed American history from the late 17th century to the present.

The girl shrugged. Should she thank him? "I just...like history."

The older man nodded, his tie moving with the force of it. It was like an abstract painting, flecks of brown and gold and blue. It made for an ugly tie, but a good place for her to train her eyes on instead of looking at him directly. "Right. The history of African Americans in this country is a fascinating one."

She had said history. She hadn't specified whose history it was that she liked. A spark of irritation lit the kindling of little stoked emotion within her and she felt the burning need to correct him. "Sure. But not nearly as fascinating as the role that religion played in the Tudor period of England. It was amazing how many people could die for their beliefs depending solely on the monarch of the time, don't you think?"

Mr. Reynolds forced a smile and said nothing as he moved away from her desk to finish handing out the rest of the papers.

"Can anyone tell me what life might have been like for a slave during the Civil War?" he asked later in the class period, his eyes skipping over her like she was a scratch on a record. It could have been worse. He could have asked her directly like some of her teachers did when black people were introduced in class, as if she could call on her ancestors and have them relay their tales to the class like some twisted version of show and tell.

The girl learned to sink a little lower in her seat then, to avert her eyes first before they had time to avert theirs or to fix them on her with a strange fascination that made her uncomfortable.

III

"Where did you come from, Cassie?" her mother often
asked with a smile.

"Your stomach," the girl replied after dinner one night,
her hands wrist deep in soapy water as she began to wash
the dishes.

"16th century England," she said another night, glasses
sliding down her nose as she glanced up from her history
textbook.

"Who knows?" Cassie sighed, halfway up the stairs on the
way to her room after another long day of school.

The answer was different every time.

Cassie sat between her mother's legs, trying to get as
comfortable as she could. In all the years that they had
taken up these exact positions, with her on the floor and
her mother on the couch, she had yet to find a way to
keep her back from hurting. Not that it mattered. She
knew that in a moment the sharp yank of the comb
through her freshly washed curls would overshadow any
back pain that she felt. Still, her mother's hands in her
hair offered her a comfort that she had yet to find
anywhere else.

"How was school?" Her mom asked.

"It was good."

IV

The girl likes Tumblr. Rather, she used to. Cute comics and fan art quickly turned into #TrayvonMartin and #MikeBrown and #blacklivesmatter. Once, she came across a list of all the names of black people killed by police in the first few months of that year. She found that she could only read some of the names before her palms began to sweat and her eyes filled with tears.

William J. Dick III, 28
Jared Forsyth, 33
Desmond Willis, 25
Richard August Hanna, 56
Alexander Myers, 23

She reblogged it and then she logged out and simply stared at the computer screen, feeling numb and angry and scared.

How many more names would be on there by the end of the year? What was to keep her name, or those of her loved ones, from being added? They all shared a similarity with the people who had been killed: brown skin.

So, she began to wear more clothes. It wasn't hard—it was cold out and she needed the extra layers. Sweaters and jeans, fuzzy socks and gloves, more and more covering until the only brown that she or anyone else could see was the brown of her face. There was little that she could do about that. She courted the thought of passing as another race, any one of the ones that had brown people, but figured that the only truly safe color was white.

V

She should have straightened her hair.

The thought is in the forefront of her mind as she watches the police car inch slowly forward, her heart picking up speed as it nears. The tag of her hoodie tickles her neck, just beneath the natural curls that she had liked so much only that morning.

She should put her hood up, hide.

No. She shouldn't.

That would only make her look suspicious. Or more suspicious, at any rate. It is late out and she is black; suspicion has already been established.

She wants to become even blacker at the moment, until she is as dark as the night and blends in with the sky, her eyes as bright as stars. She wants to step into the world of fiction and borrow an invisibility cloak that she can wrap tightly around herself. She has her own You-Know-Who to hide from. She can hear what her mother would have to say, hear the notes of reproach in her voice, the exasperation as she tries to instill some confidence in the girl. The girl looks for it now, somewhere in the crushed leaves and the yellowing grass but all she can see are her own footprints. She stares at the ground as if she has forgotten the glow of the moon and the stars in the sky or the glare of the headlights too close for comfort.

When she blinks out of her reverie it is to find the cop car parked beside her, its passenger side window slowly inching downward as her own anxiety mounts.

She must put on a smile for the people who kill men like her father and boys younger than her brother.

"Are those donuts for us?" they ask. They are smiling.
They seem friendly. They are only campus cops. She
does not make any sudden movements.

"No." The girl keeps her smile in place, hating herself.
Yes, she wants to say. Take them and please don't shoot
me. "But you can buy some. My roommate plays rugby
and they're having a fundraiser."

The men in blue nod, even chuckle a little. "Have a good
night," they say, dismissing her. She goes. On her way up
to her room she throws the box of donuts in the trash.

Sometimes I Cry
Antwon

My daughter's smile weighs heavy on my heart
So heavy that I'm sitting here crying in the dark
Repeatedly telling myself, "Twon, you should have tried
harder"
"Twon, you should have been a better father"
I mean I was so into the street life
That I couldn't see how my actions were affecting my
child's life
Was I that caught up that I forgot my own daughter's
worth?
You see I know I messed up and it hurts
There is no excuse I can give her to explain my absence
Yet I still need for her to understand all that was
happening
From my hungry days to my lonely nights
I want her to get a good picture of my life
In the hope that she will believe my truth and not the
world's lies
I am not afraid to say that
Sometimes I cry

Symphony
Joanna Heaney

Symphony
Prosecutor strides up
"Ladies and gentlemen of the jury"
Grips the podium
And begins.
—

A symphony unfolds
Clarinets sob shrill cries
"The suspect's innocent, my son's a good boy!"
But this piece is already written
—

Trumpets scream out
Drown the cries
"HE DESERVES IT"
And the drumbeats grow louder.
—

Gavel strikes the cymbal
20 years sentenced in a grand crash
The prosecutor sways in rapture,
The symphony concluded.

Second Chances
Khalid Karim

I should've loved her better
and her absence is a constant ache to my soul
but even when I try, I can't forget her.
She was always there,
morning, noon, and night,
and her presence alone was tender love and care.
And still I took it for granted
as if she'd always be there.
Thinking she'd love me unconditionally
and listening to that old cliché
had me mistreating her foolishly.
And mistaking her compassion for ignorance,
I continued to treat her stupidly
but she has standards
and rightfully demanded more of me.
Still I left her,
she didn't abandon me
but she's smarter than you think
and won't take me back so easily.
But I swear that I'm a changed man now
because of this tragedy,
becoming what she needed and wanted badly,
if she'd have me.
I no longer want to be apart. I want to be one
and promise to be dedicated and upright
if you'd only have me... Freedom

The Woman in the Mirror
Hricko

I've never been one to gaze in the mirror. I have friends
who can do it for hours. Maybe they have high self-
esteem, or maybe they are vain, I can't say. I used to look
in the mirror and see only my flaws. I didn't like my hair,
my teeth, my eyes or some other part of my face. Don't
get me started on the ways I was dissatisfied with my body.
But that was all before I committed my crime. That is
when my simple dislike for myself became pure self-
loathing.

The first part of my incarceration was spent in the state's
forensic hospital, Clifton T. Perkins. There aren't any real
mirrors in the maximum security wing but I would still
occasionally catch a glimpse of myself in a piece of safety
glass. "I hate myself" was the first thing I would think
upon seeing any part of myself. I often said it out loud. I
wanted to disappear and I tried, but the staff at Perkins
diligently prevented that. I can appreciate that now, but
back then I was only angry.

An even more reprehensible version of my would appear
on the Plexiglas encased television in the dayroom.
Seventeen years later, I can clearly remember the feeling.
Nearly every day the news report would misunderstand
me, that a perpetrator suffers is not wrong but it should
not be from a truth that festers inside of her. Not when
that truth can bring healing to a victim or help rebuild a
community. We have to do better. I have to do better.

Now I look at myself in the mirror and see someone that
is real and I do not hate her any more. In reaching
beyond myself and trying to heal victims I have found a

way to heal myself. The more I heal, the more I can give.
And I will.

25

No Rest for the Wicked
Marisa Fein

Sometimes, it sounds like rain,
a downpour, torrential
that leaves my eyes
sticky with sleep.

Last week, it was the sound
a body makes when it
slams into water-
a crack and a flood.

Tonight, it is this:
metal on metal,
a guard who yells
"welfare checks!"
every half hour

Every
    half hour.

I am suspended
between this reality of
rain and glass,
a car crash
without impact.

In this cell of exhaustion,
I am a prisoner of their
metal induced insomnia.

Gold Stars Never Die
Anna Hassanyeh

On a warm summer evening, when I was twelve years old, my dad said to me, "writing's for pansies and the pretentious, Anthony boy." My dad had a way of conveying his own brand of parental wisdom with such certainty that I wanted to believe him.

He passed me the piece of paper I'd shown him, a poem I'd copied out at school that day, with a kind comment and a gold star from my English teacher, Mr. Carter. My dad un-tucked his shirt from his jeans, kicked off his slide-sandals and collapsed on the couch letting out a long breath, like air bleeding from a car tire. He took a bottle of Budweiser from the ice bucket, broke the cap off with his teeth and spat it onto the floor. Mr. Carter taught poetry and stories with irresistible passion and believed that anyone could be a writer. So, that evening, I told my dad that I would be a writer, if I got enough gold stars. After I told him, I folded the poem in half and wedged it between the couch cushions beside a stolen watch and a few dollars of some kid's lunch money. I don't recall my dad's reply. Some parts of my childhood I remember clearly, but not enough to create a complete picture. The memories I have retained are the days I spent with Tiffany swaggering around town like the law was our foe and we were the righteous. But that was a long time ago.

It was a few years after I was lawfully grown, when the temperature was edging towards a hot summer, that I found myself sitting with three other inmates in the prison education facility. The room we were in was gray, with metal desks in lines, facing a flip chart with no paper to flip. There was a mustached correctional officer sitting on a plastic chair in the corner, dressed in blue, arms crossed over his bulging belly, bored as hell.

O'Leary, the only inmate I'd taken a liking to, talked me into coming after I happened to mention I made up stories and poems as a kid. What'd you got to lose? he'd said.

O'Leary had a voice that was soft and slow, as if he put the weight of the world onto every word. He was small, pale and stringy looking. His teeth were rotten to the jawbone, which he would complain about night and day.

He told me his appearance was a permanent affliction caused by a childhood of chronic neglect and an adulthood of everything that was unlawful and unholy. After my first few months at the penitentiary, I didn't need to ask what kind of life people lived, I just had to see the marks on their skin, the look in their eyes, the way they walked and talked. I knew them before I even met them and they knew me.

I sat on a desk next to O'Leary who was trying to break the flexible prison pen the officer had given him. I couldn't remember the last time I wrote something, maybe a telephone number or a signature for a bank loan. Usually, in prison, the only ink you saw was on your fingertips.

I wrote my name at the top of the lined paper. Tiffany used to sit next to me in school and she'd write her name with curly loops that sat on the line, the tip of her pen gliding against the page. I wrote mine with hard capitals, like rigid sticks.

I stared at my name: ANTHONY WARNER. I drew
stars around it because I wanted to be reminded that stars
still existed.

"Hi, everyone." The woman that walked into the room
was short and fat, with a face that smiled too much. Her
hair was so unnaturally coiffed you'd have thought she'd
just walked out of the hair salon. She was wearing
everything black except for a pair of pink-rimmed glasses,
which dangled from a gold chain around her neck and
swayed from the cliff of her large breasts. "We have
another writer joining us, today," she said.

I wondered who this other writer was until I noticed the
woman was staring at me.

"Welcome, Mr. Warner." She smiled.

I nodded.

"I'm Ms. Bishop. Who can remind us what we talked
about last session?" Her voice was high-pitched, like one
of those little yappy dogs that rich city women carry
around.

"What makes a good piece of writing," O'Leary said.

"Correct," Ms. Bishop replied.

Jackson started cracking his fingers.

"If you keep popping them bones, you'll get the arthritis,"
Ramos said, his bug-eyes sticking out like a bloated toad.

"My abuelo got the arthritis," he added.

Ms. Bishop handed me a course booklet.
Ramos continued: "His hands got all claw like and ugly
looking. It was so bad, he couldn't even pick up a pen."
Ramos held his bendy pen above his head and slammed
it on to the table. Jackson stopped cracking.

"Thank you, Mr. Ramos, maybe you'd like to write about
your abuelo in today's class, because we're going to be
exploring characterization." Ms. Bishop put on her pink
glasses, licked her right index finger and flicked through
the pages of her booklet.

"Turn to page 4," she said.

There was a list of questions writers would ask themselves
to help them work out their characters. Ms. Bishop read
them aloud. There were stupid questions like:

What does your character have in his/her refrigerator?
What does he/she have on his/her bedside table?

Unless you were writing about what someone's got in their
refrigerator, or on their bedside table, who'd give a shit.

After Ms. Bishop finished reading, she glanced at the
clock on the opposite side of the room. "You have 20
minutes to write about a character or someone you know
using the questions to help you."

Ramos began to write; his pen made quick ticking sounds.

Jackson cracked his fingers, wrote a sentence, cracked a
finger, and wrote a sentence. Cracked his neck: left crack,
right crack.

I turned to O'Leary; his handwriting was neat and loopy.

I wasn't comfortable making up a character and the only person I could write about was Tiffany. Tiffany and I are the same age, born in the same town; we grew up together. She has pale skin and doesn't go out much in the sun because she'd cook like a cracked egg on a hot sidewalk. Tiffany would have half-eaten candy bars in her refrigerator and a pile of books on her bedside table.

"Ten minutes left," Ms. Bishop said.

My hands were hot and sticky against the rubber body of the pen. Under my name and the stars, I wrote: TIFFANY. The more I looked at my writing the more I realized I shouldn't be here. I drew stars around Tiffany's name.

"Eight minutes," Ms. Bishop said.

I drew stars along the rest of the line.

"Five minutes."

I kept drawing stars; they got bigger and bigger, darker and darker, until the whole page was filled with the damn things.

"Pens down," Ms. Bishop said.

Ramos slammed his pen onto the table. Jackson cracked his wrist whilst turning it in lazy circles. O'Leary continued to write and I covered my paper so no one could see what I'd done.

The chatter at supper in the dining hall rose to what sounded like a baritone of barking and snarling dogs.

Ground beef with brown gravy, dry mashed potatoes and canned sweet corn was on the menu that day. Two inmates across the hall started to push each like big kids fighting over an ice pop.

"What'd you write about?" O'Leary asked me.

"Nothing much." I shrugged.

"You read books and talk big words, writing should be easy for you."

"O'Leary, I talk shit and have no ideas worth writing about."

O'Leary finished his meal and placed his spoon in the middle of his tray like he was in a fancy restaurant.

"You looking forward to freedom?" he asked.

"I can't wait to see Tiffany. I swear it's like I'm being reborn." I held my arms up to the ceiling and hollered, "Hallelujah!"

* * *

Jackson was cracking his knuckles and the clock on the classroom wall was ticking behind its own set of bars. Ms. Bishop glanced at the blank lined paper beneath my poised pen.

We were learning about dialogue and had twenty minutes to write a scene using speech. The only talk I thought to write about was on a hot afternoon in August, about seven years ago, when I was driving Tiffany to the 7-Eleven in my dad's old truck. Tiffany was wearing a black t-shirt, camouflage mini-skirt and high-top sneakers, and had a

head full of curls that rippled like flames whenever she
turned her head.

"You got the list?" I asked.

"All up in here, Anthony boy." She tapped her freckled
forehead.

"Impressive." I laughed.

She laughed, too, all white teeth and pink gums, like she
was posing for a photograph.

I parked the truck outside the store.

"Leave the engine running," she said.

A few minutes later we were back in the truck and
speeding along the highway. Tiffany had the window
open, which made her curls wilder than the wind blowing
through them.

"Anthony boy, that's the last time we're doing that," she
said, taking a packet of Skittles from the pocket of her
skirt and adding it to the collection of stolen Coke cans
and candy bars. Her blue eyes absorbed the sunlight
making them sparkle like rough crystals.

"You always say that." I sighed with mock exasperation
because there was nothing Tiffany could do to annoy me.
That's what I thought at the time.

"Stealing is like taking drugs. You start small-time, then
end up getting lost in the big stuff." She opened a can of
Coke.

I parked the truck beside a playground that had bunches
of flowers tied to the gate. Tiffany stared at the empty
swings.

"We gotta grow up sometime, Anthony boy."

Writing time was up and I'd got another piece of paper
filled with stars. Ramos was swinging on his chair, leaning
his head back so he was looking at me upside down.
"What you gonna write for the assignment?" he asked
me.

Ms. Bishop had mentioned a writing assignment in last
week's class, which was due a week before I was to be
released. I hadn't given it much thought and that's what I
told Ramos. His front chair legs hit the wooden floor and
he turned to look at me straight on. The serpent tattoo on
this shaved head moved with the tensing of his jaw.

"I'm gonna write about prison, ya know? Write about the
hard stuff." Ramos's eyes bugged out and I could see the
crazy in them. "I'm getting published." He grinned and
stuck his tongue out like a panting dog.

Ms. Bishop returned our previous work. I saw the lines of
stars I'd drawn. Squeezed into the margin, Ms. Bishop
had written:

*"When I, sitting, heard the astronomer, where he
lectured with such applause in the lecture room,
How soon, unaccountable, I became tired and sick;
Till rising and gliding out, I wander'd off by myself,
In the mystical moist night-air, and from time to time,
Look'd up in perfect silence at the stars." – Walt
Whitman*

Heat slithered up my spine and twisted itself around each rib. I stood with the paper in my hand and walked towards the door.

"You can't leave the facility without supervision," the officer in the corner said.

"I need the bathroom."

There's the remnant of an old crack in the door, plastered and painted thick. The tense heat was now in my throat and I was scared it would pour out of my eyes.

"Sit down," the officer said. This time he stood and walked towards me, his breath in my face. One breathe, two breaths, three breaths. I turned and sat down.

* * *

I was sitting in the prison lobby in the same clothes I was wearing when they brought me in 5 years ago: jeans, sneakers, a Pink Floyd t-shirt that still smelled of sweat and marijuana.

The day before, as I packed, O'Leary lectured me about second chances and Ms. Bishop said she'd give me an extension on my writing assignment, which I hadn't even started. She said I could mail it to her, if I wanted.

I almost smiled when my dad walked through the automatic doors. His slide sandals flip flapped against the bottom of his feet and an unlit cigarette hung from his lips.

When he saw me he said, "Come on then, Anthony boy."

We were sat in the old truck. My dad was driving. A few strands of his hair glinted gray in the sunlight.

"What you gonna do now?" he asked.

"I'm gonna grab a burger and fries," I said and my dad chuckled loud and deep. "And then I'm gonna see Tiffany."

He stopped the truck on the side of the road and cut the ignition.

"You remember your mother?"

"Yes," I replied. When I was eight years old, my mom killed herself driving drunk. Took an old man and his dog up to heaven with her. I don't recall much during that time.

"You remember how some days she was your mother and other days she was mad as hell?" my dad continued, looking up at the sky through the front window of the truck. The heat from the hood made the air melt. "You'd be as mad as your mother if you go anywhere near Tiffany; you'll be back in the slammer, as fast as that." He clicked his fingers.

I woke the next morning at 8.00am and thought about O'Leary and the others eating breakfast from gray prison trays. My bowl was white and round and chipped on the edges. I leaned against the kitchen counter and ate cereal with day old milk. Everything was the same: the same couch, the same ice bucket filled to tipping with beer bottles.

I drove to the 7-Eleven and bought a Coke and a packet
of Skittles. I sat in the truck outside Tiffany's house,
which hadn't changed: manicured lawn, a porch with two
wooden pots with spiky plants, which brushed against
people's clothes whenever they walked by.

I ate the red Skittles and left the other colors. As I
cracked open a Coke, Tiffany's screen door opened and
a young boy, about four years old, ran onto the porch. He
was wearing denim overalls tucked into galoshes. His hair
was a sandy color and his cheeks were flushed pink. He
clutched a toy dog and was sucking his thumb. I then saw
Tiffany. She hadn't changed since the last time I saw her,
in a courtroom, six years ago. Beautiful.

I'll never forget what she said to the judge that day and the
relief on her face when I was sentenced: no more
Anthony boy following her around town; no more
Anthony boy calling her late at night; no more Anthony
boy waiting outside her house, waiting and waiting. No
more Anthony boy posting threatening notes, and no
more Anthony boy holding her down, holding a knife
with his top lip sweating. She'll never forget that, she said.

When Tiffany saw me in the truck, she took the child by
the arm and pulled him back into the house with her.
The screen door clattered shut and the jalousies quivered.

I ate the rest of the Skittles and drove home.

I watched daytime chat shows until my dad returned from
cleaning pools. We ate takeaway pizza with the glare of
the TV on our faces. He fell asleep on the couch, feet on
the coffee table, head back, and mouth open. The air
conditioner attached to the window hummed even though
I'd turned it off hours before.

I stood out on the porch because the air was warm even though the stars were out and I was reminded of the summer evening when I was twelve and the poem I put between the couch cushions. I smoked a cigarette and drank a bottle of beer and made it last until the sky began to lighten.

My dad was no longer on the couch, so I searched between the cushions. I found a couple of dimes, a pen, the stolen watch stuck on four o'clock and a piece of folded paper. I unfolded it, careful, as it was weak at the creases. I read the words of the Walt Whitman poem, the same poem Ms. Bishop wrote on my work. I couldn't make out Mr .Carter's faded comment, but the gold star shone just as bright.

There were piles of gas and electricity bills and discarded empty envelopes on the kitchen table. I took one of the envelopes and wrote my name on it to see if the pen still worked. It did. The wooden chair creaked as I sat and I thought of Ramos writing about his time in prison, about his life and the hard stuff. I thought of O'Leary writing about what he'd do if he were given a second chance. I knew then what I wanted to write, so I placed the pen nib to the envelope, and this is what I wrote.

Last Meal
Emily Paulsrud

A condemned man's last meal
Window to his soul

Here's the apple juice
A reminder of all the mornings
The mornings without juice
Without a parent who cared
An empty table
An empty stomach
An empty heart

Here's the hamburger
American through-and-through
A slice of freedom
In a world of confinement
Irony you can taste

Here's the ice cream
A sweet relief
From the heat of a youth
Spent in the embrace
Of violence
New mother for an unloved child

Here's the bread
"My body given for you"
A sacrifice on the altar
Of an unforgiving society

Here's the body
Not fried but raw
Raw pain

Raw indifference

Meat grinded by the system
Prepared for years
And put to death
Right around the time
Meals are served
On family's tables
All over the country

Please No Cheating!
Maureen Geraghty & Jevon Jackson

"You Americans, you are so naïve. You think evil is going
to come into your houses wearing big black boots. It
doesn't come like that. Look at the language. It begins in
the language." - Russian poet, Joseph Brodsky

Maureen:

He's been moved from a maximum to a medium security
prison. Jevon's stellar record as an inmate for the past
twenty-two years earns him this status (or is it that the
maximum-security prison is overcrowded and the powers
that be need to move bodies? No one knows). The men
housed in the medium-security prisons have more out-of-
cell time, more access to resources such as the library, the
gym, and the dayroom (where they can use the phone to
call loved ones) than those housed in maximum security.
One opportunity offered at the new facility is a college
math class, which he signed up for right away. He's a
reading and writing guy so math would be a challenge, a
potential skill he could hone for his betterment and
rehabilitation.

After taking a test and receiving a qualifying score for
entry into the class, he is assigned a teacher. On day one,
this teacher sets the tone. She lectures the inmate
students, "this is a college class. You can't be late or skip.
You will be expected to do the work assigned." These
are fair and appropriate expectations for college students,
he thinks. He is anxious to begin. After a few days of pre-
tests, text books get handed out and they review. He feels
ready to move on, enough review already. He is patient

because that is what prison requires, so he generalizes the art of waiting to the classroom.

For the next few weeks, the teacher goes over the first two chapters in the text while in class. Finally, the teacher hands out the first homework assignment. He takes his college math, returns to his cell ready to work. When he pulls out the paper, he notices something across the top of the assignment. In bright red Sharpie the teacher writes, "PLEASE NO CHEATING!" A familiar queasiness, the taste of copper in his mouth. He expects this dismissive remark from prison guards, but from a teacher? Tomorrow he will say something to her but he has to perfectly plan his approach. Make sure he is prepared so his words cannot be twisted into something later used against him. These mental gymnastics are required in dealing with people who treat him less than human, expect the worst, feel that power is meant to belittle.

He enters the class the next day and as opportunity affords, asks the teacher, calmly, "excuse me, are you going to write this on all of our assignments?" He inches toward the condescension at hand.

"Yes, I am. Is there a problem?" the teacher answers flatly. "This is offensive. Why write this on every assignment?" He is both curious and stern.

"I don't want you guys helping each other with the work," she mumbles as she looks away, acting busy stacking papers.

He cocks his head in confusion. "Well, instead of 'PLEASE NO CHEATING!' why don't you write 'NO HELPING EACH OTHER!' or somethin' like that?"

The teacher tightens her jaw and responds, defensively, "that would be too much to write out."
Even she knows her answer makes no sense, sounds lame. He throws her an analogy, attempts to get her to empathize without becoming combative, "how would you feel if every day when you come to work, your boss warns you, 'DON'T STEAL ANYTHING!'?"

At this, the teacher has no response. She's been challenged by her student, the inmate in College Math 107, and she has nothing to say to save her. She looks away, mumbles, "don't take it personally. This is just how I do things." She pivots at the lectern and goes on to scribble math problems on the whiteboard.

He has already blocked her out. He hears nothing for the rest of the class except his own siren thoughts. While she speaks fractions, he brainstorms a withdrawal letter that he will later articulately pound out for the educational director.

"PLEASE NO CHEATING!"— one more red flag of failure. Another "innocent" remark bold with subtext screaming unworthiness, disrespect. A psychological kick in the head masked as "just how things are done." One class, three college credits, thirty eight years of not being treated "personally." Do the math.

Jevon—

A few days after writing to the educational director, she called me down to her office. We talked for about twenty minutes, and she was receptive, professional and considerate. I explained that the "PLEASE NO CHEATING!" admonishment written at the top of every assignment was really a priming, a negative pre-

conditioning that was offensive and completely
unnecessary in a classroom setting where grown adult
men had eagerly volunteered to take the class. Although
we were convicts, not one of us in class had given the
teacher any indication (by habit or attitude) that we were
prone to cheat. I elaborated on the various university
studies that had been done to show how such negative
pre-conditioning, in a classroom setting, can have a
marked correlation to students' lower test scores. The
director was forthcoming in that she had a bias toward her
colleague, the math teacher, whom she'd worked with for
years. She said that she looked at the "PLEASE NO
CHEATING!" statement as "harmless;" but she did
assure me that she would give the issue to her supervisor
to look into. She also asked if there were any other issues
and I explained that this math teacher didn't want to pass
back our pre-tests that we took a month ago and,
therefore, we had no idea of our individual strengths and
weaknesses. The director informed me she would
address all the issues and that I should file a formal
grievance if, within the next week, my concerns were not
resolved.

As I got up to leave, the director tried to hand the
assignment in question back to me. I told her I wanted
her to pass it on to her supervisor so he/she could see the
letters glowing at the top of the page like a cheap Las
Vegas casino neon sign. It was important to capture the
visual of the disrespect firsthand.

Within the next week, the math teacher begrudgingly
passed back to us the month-old pre-tests. As she weaved
between the rows of desks, she shook her head, annoyed.
"This is the part that I hate—I really don't like handing
things back." She then handed out a second homework
assignment and to my delight, there was no "PLEASE

NO CHEATING!" written at the top. Finally, my voice had been heard. Someone, somewhere, with the authority to restore a measure of decorum back to the teacher-student power dynamic, had issued a decree to force this uncompromising math teacher to change her "way of doing things." But my silent celebration was short lived. As the teacher finished handing out the assignment to everyone, she began a scolding sermon about how the class was for our own benefit and how she wouldn't force us to do the work. She went on to state that "some" of the class hadn't turned in the first assignment and that if people were serious about their education, they'd have to be willing to do the work. She then lasered in on me—I was the "some" she was referring to—and standing in front of the entire class she asked, "Mr. Jackson, are you going to complete this assignment?"

I could feel everyone's eyes on me. This was one of those spotlight moments that defines who you are as a person—when you're caught completely off-guard, you have no polished, prepared response, no choreographed reaction, and you can feel your heartbeat in the gulp of your throat. I wanted to respond with a scathing diatribe on how I have a right, as a human being, to "take it personally" when an educator assumes I'm prone to cheat. I wanted to rifle out sentiments of how my self-respect is more important than irrational numbers and Pythagorean theorems, and that it was not okay to casually dismiss such disrespect, particularly when the disrespect has been seamlessly ingrained into the status quo. I wanted to say a lot of things, but what actually came out of my mouth, after she threw the spotlight on me, was a calm and concise response, "Yeah, I'll do the assignment as long as you don't write that stuff at the top of the paper."

After class, one of my classmates asked me, puzzled, "What was that all about?"

"Nothin'," I said. "A whole lot of nothin'."

A day or two later, the math teacher was going over problems on the whiteboard, explaining why we had to show our work—showing all the steps and calculations that led us to the answer, when she made a comment about how she didn't want us to "cheat ourselves." She then stopped abruptly and said, "Oh, I can't say that word. 'Cheating'—that's a bad word." With her fingers, she made a zipping motion across her lips. "I don't want to get in trouble... can't use that word."

She never looked directly at me when she said this, but it was clear that her big, invisible passive-aggressive assault rifle had just let off a couple rounds in my direction. I didn't say anything. In my mind, I tried to not allow her attitude to negatively affect my desire to learn. But, in the succeeding days, I could feel my attention evaporate in that class. The math textbook began to feel as if it weighed one hundred pounds. I'm a nerd by nature, so I've always loved school. I'm the guy who goes to the library and checks out psychology textbooks "for fun". So when the always thriving desire to learn began to wither away inside of me like a brown, crinkled autumn leaf three days before winter, I knew I had to absolutely withdraw from that class. Which I ultimately did a few weeks later. Not only was this teacher baiting me with passive-aggressive behavior, likely with the expectation that I'd respond by saying something disrespectful to justify exacting a penalty or punishment upon me, but she was also a very ineffective math instructor. I went over her head to her supervisor with my grievance and she was forced to change her way of doing things. Even in her silence, she continued to remind me of her displeasure.

As a prisoner, I have to deal with irreverent and obnoxious guards every day. I can't get away from them. But a disrespectful and disgruntled math teacher—I can choose to remove that kind of drama from my already constricted life.

I've talked to a number of different people about his "PLEASE NO CHEATING!" thing and a lot of people's initial reaction is: "what's the big deal?" or "you know you're not cheating, so just ignore it." And this is exactly how such harmful and detrimental things (bias, discrimination, negative pre-conditioning) become systematically woven into the status quo. Nobody effectively challenges them. Too many people concede to the minor slights and offenses, which then, over time, grow into solid, immovable forces. What compounded this specific situation, for me, was when I initially presented the issue in a calm, respectful manner, directly to the teacher, her immediate attitude was dismissive. I was ignored as 'business as usual'. I had no doubt that such a practice of writing, "PLEASE NO CHEATING!" on the top of any college assignment would not be tolerated in the free world. So why was it permissible with prisoners? Because of the great fixed force of indifference that abounds within the walls of these prisons. This is what I have continued to fight against throughout various aspects of my incarceration- systematic disregard and deliberate disregard by staff and administrators. It surprised me to see that it could reach the sacred space of the classroom. This is why situations like this have to be challenged when they are small and barely perceivable—to prevent this indifference from getting out of hand. To not challenge it, to fail to name it for the inhumane beast that it is, we would only be cheating ourselves.

Maureen-

I couldn't help thinking that Jevon's treatment by his college teacher was not an isolated prison story. It made me wonder how many hundreds of "PLEASE NO CHEATING!" slights happened in schools years before these men went to prison. How many of the "it's not a big deal" or "don't take it personally" justifications paved a slow, subtle road of low expectation, failure, expulsion, or worse?

I can't imagine a teacher that would consider it normal or innocent to put such a daunting, negative warning on every assignment given to a student. Unfortunately, I believe this educational form of racial profiling happens regularly and systematically in the same seemingly benign ways as a red Sharpie warning.

Ta-Nehisi Coates says in his book, *Between the World and Me*, "I came to see the streets and the schools as arms of the same beast. One enjoyed the official power of the state while the other enjoyed its implicit sanctions... And I began to see these two arms in relation—those who failed the schools justified their failures in the streets. The society could say, 'he should have stayed in school.' and then wash their hands of him."

Both Coates and Jevon's stories are sirens, spotlights on institutionalized discrimination that hides (and often stands blatantly apparent) in our nation's schools. As teachers, we must question what is stated or implied in our "just the way we do things." If knowledge is truly power, if education is truly liberation and even

rehabilitation, we have a moral imperative to put our
curriculum and our modes of instruction under a
microscope to see clearly and through a diverse lens.
WE must slay the beasts of injustice and purge prejudices
in our classrooms starting with the language.

*Authors Note: Jevon and I have been corresponding for
over 20 years. We met while I was teaching in a juvenile
detention center in Milwaukee, Wisconsin when he was
16, before he was ultimately waived into adult court and
given a life prison sentence. This piece is a part of a larger
work-in-progress that speaks to the power of writing and
redemption as well as the social injustices embedded in
the American prison and education systems.

This article was inspired by the multitude of professional
development trainings that launched my teaching year
focusing on topics such as Courageous Conversations,
Diversity in the Classroom, Closing the Achievement
Gap, and Restorative Justice. The difference between
theory and practice was so glaring in Jevon's experience,
whether between prison or school walls, the story seemed
worthy of exposure.

I Was Mistaken
Kimberly Hricko

There's no way you could be
As bad as everyone said.
I thought, they must not know you
Like I know you.
But I was mistaken.

I believed it when you said
That you care about me
When you said that you wouldn't hurt me
I thought I'd found a real friend.
But I was mistaken.

I hoped that you saw
The kindness, beauty and value in me
But I was mistaken.
You saw something
That appealed to you
In that moment.
But moments pass.

I believed I was done
Making stupid choices.
I thought I was done losing,
No more lessons to learn.
But I was mistaken.

I thought I was strong,
Safely behind my wall.
But I was mistaken.
What I am, is numb,
Tired and bone weary.

They say that there's
No shame in making one.
They say that mistakes
Are opportunities to learn. I thought my slowness
To trust someone again was
A bad thing.
But again, I was mistaken.

Crocus Reborn
Alfred "Spoken Truth"

Beneath the spoiling earth
The vernal harbingering my coming
Vitality warmth awakens my core
Lobed 4 expansion, my seed intermitting multiple spasms
Vibrating my ovaries
My stamen point northward contracting
Flower shooting the longitudinal ladder 2 ecstasy-
endosperm
My antlers spread outwards acting as antennas
Attracting pollen 4 the reproduction phases of this
plantation
My third eye enhanced by a rainbow collection of colors
Yellow, blue, purple, crimson, prevailing who I am
Crocus, The Flower Reborn!
Finally, I've broken through the soil, nutrient deficiency
My stigma projecting, caught by the face of the storm
Concrete mixed wit gravel, scarred my foliage section
Like the Rose, I secrete blood from my damaged petals
Here I stand, in the hell winds of my Botanical Garden
Tossed 2 & fro, observing infestation of pesticide, weed
and fungus
Back I am, Crocus, The Flower Reborn!
Encouraging champion males 2 fight 4 the cause!
Poppy got shot while unarmed!
Daisy got date-raped in a college dorm
Sweet pea selling her body dope fiending
At the same time attracting sexually transmitted potato
disease
White Dead Nettle & Black Rose exposed the world 2
race issues
All Lotus wants is a bridge between the two

Platooning in the streets, peacefully protesting, "We're all equal!"
How is it, we provide oxygen, but these bad crops have taken our right 2 breathe?
Male Sheld Fern, protect our right 2 live!
May the sunshine reveal these ill mentalities
Stop the brutalities
Whether it be economically or socially
We need education 2 succeed
Or epidemically our youth will be affected by a disease poverty
Constantly warring wit triumph vs. tragedy
A war that seems 2 have no ending
But I'm back from the beginning in the form of
Crocus The Flower, reborn 2 birth enlightenment 2 mental darkness
A spokesperson 4 the down-trodden who's lost and forgotten
Battle tested by the elements in this bloom cycle
Like yours, my stem is sore, petals bandaged
But I refuse 2 fall over from winter's harshness
Never broken! Spring inspired, birth 2 endure reason and purpose
And from my resilience, I sprout 2 tell my story
Cultivating life from the lifeless
Never glorified, but humbled by intelligence
Understanding the difference in climates temporal by law
Anger brings summer heat, violent brush fires
Seeds fall 2 earth surface hurt, cuffed by thorn wires
Winter processes be long unjust prison sentences
Spring produces, freedom, justice, equality fragrances
But we're still grieving, demanding swift answers
2 why our beautiful bouquet is still being displayed
At wakes and funerals!
Crocus The Flower Reborn!

Stirring Deep Waters
Josef Krebs

Stirring deep waters
I upset the silt
Reintroducing dust into the flow of things

Best left settled
Undisturbed and un-disturbing
Instead of floating with potential
Of collision

Being that best left forgotten
If not un-affecting
Just by its presence
Or the knowledge thereof

Singularly lost
As we all must be
Adrift

Starring at the Wall
Curtis

I was warned there'd be times like these
But nothing could've prepared me for Dr. Swartz
Who comes around once a week
Peeking in my cell like he knows me better than I know
myself
I'll bet he gets a kick out of seeing a twenty-two year old
Who has been locked away in a cell since he was 16
Who has thirty more to go if a blessing doesn't come
through this damn wall
That he's been starring at for the past six hours
I often come to this wall to somewhat free my mind
Or to drown out my annoying cellie
Who can't stop talking about his boring relationship with
his girlfriend he can't seem to stop fighting
Even though she calls the cops on him every time
Or sometimes when the lights go out and the prison
raucous is done for the day
I guess to seek mental refuge from this place
Other times just to reflect on what life was like before 23
and 1*
When it was cookouts, Huggies and hamburgers
Yeah, that always brings a smile to my face
Lately that's been the routine
I start reflecting and end up with this smile
Starring at this damn wall!
Then here comes this Dr. wanting to know why I'm sitting
here smiling at the wall
I give him the usual "nothing"
But to be honest
I smile to keep from crying

*23 and 1 - solitary confinement

21 Guns
Dimitri

Stuck in this world
Where I feel so all alone
Froze on face, a cold stare
Like the arctic was my home
Keep calling on God
But he never answers the phone
Where else am I supposed to turn
When a house is not a home?
Six feet deep
Is the only time I'll sleep
'Cause if you close ya eyes once
Then the devil surely creeps
Black birds on the sill
But they never make a peep
Eager vultures on the watch
Waiting on the lost of feet
Feel my pain
Like aching bones from when it rains
It's a permanent strain
Wish I could get out of this game
Where everyone loses
And the winner becomes insane
I welcome a quick death
21 guns scream bang, bang!!

Writing Inside
Kimberly Hricko

When I write, I allow myself freedom to remember things
that would otherwise be too scary or painful. I am locked
up and there is also the sadness of loss attached to even
my happiest memories. Yet in the act of writing I find
wholeness. I can unearth the parts of my life that I keep
most hidden and once they are set on paper I can plumb
the solace and peace of my own depths. Writing is my gift
to myself.

In front of a typewriter, computer terminal or notebook, I
am safe to strip away my armor. The layers of intellect,
humor and aloofness that serve me all day long don't
serve me when I write. The din of my noisy prison
surroundings fades away. Hundreds of rules that dictate
my behavior disappear. There is no razor wire. There is
no life sentence. No line to wait in, no pass to show.
Within this crazy, harsh environment I create my most
private intimacy.

I have discovered that here is a great well of sadness
within me. It is the anchor that holds me down, it keeps
me from floating out into the universe. The shape and the
weight of this melancholy define me. When I write, I am
able to touch this black mass. I can finger its edges and
palm its heft, put my cheek against its cold surface. In
writing here, while I am confined, I do not write to
exorcise this sadness, but rather to absorb it.

On paper words shock me. It is as if my fingers on the
keyboard know better how and what I feel than my brain
ever has. They recognize what my heart cannot bear. The
paper does no judge me; the notebook calmly accepts my

burdens without complaint. The shame of my childhood sexual abuse was something I couldn't tolerate speaking about until I wrote it.

And if the sadness that I write from doesn't turn to happiness like Oprah or Dr. Phil say it should, that is okay too, because it is mine. Because I was brave enough to tell it.

Forgotten
Joanna Heaney

46 years old
15 spent on death row
Taken without batting an eyelash
—

Beaten in a cell
Frozen in winter
Boiling in summer
—

Strip-searched on a whim
Ignored 23 hours a day
Forgotten
—

When the inmate dies?
Newspapers mourn the loss
And society forgets again.

Hunting for Answers
Rafael

As I sit looking through the window
Consumed with finding the source of my emotions

I feel anger, sorrow, regret, and yet with all my pondering
I can't seem to pinpoint the reason for all the commotion

Am I angry because of my actions and choices in the
past?

Or is it because I'm secluded from the people I hold dear
to my heart, secluded from their smiles and laughs?

Do I feel sorrow because I can't be there to be a brother,
or son, or a friend and lover to some lucky one?

Maybe the origin of my sorrow is from me getting up
everyday
And feeling lonelier with every setting of the sun

Could the regret that I feel crawl from where I'm at and
where I could've been?

Possibly, I beat myself up over the fact that I regret so
much and don't move on and forget about that stuff like
trash in a trash bin.

I'm sitting with unfocused eyes
Paralyzed in the hunt for my answers

In the Name of Safety
Emily Paulsrud

61

Step out of line
Do some time
In the name of safety

Lines drawn and re-drawn
Impossible to keep track
In the name of safety

Men and women vilified
System feeling justified
In the name of safety

Inescapable record
Modernity's chain gang
In the name of safety

Families separated
Humanities destroyed
In the name of safety

We are all accountable
(In the name of safety)

Shattered
Kimberly Hricko

A billion pieces of my life
lay shattered,
scattered
and forsaken.

I cut myself trying
to gather them up
as if fixing them
were an option.

My destruction is total.
Shunned and alone
I sit at my personal ground zero.

Only pain and despair
fill the void left
by my ruin.

I am everything they say I am.
Failure, worthless, criminal.

My only relief
is a frightening suicidal clarity.
When there is not hope
tomorrow is a curse.

Yet the smallest flame
a desire to survive
remains deep in my belly.
I shall endure.

Drunks: Indian Country, New Mexico
Rick Lyon

Report Drunk Drivers, the signs say
as if ubiquitous roadside crosses don't,
pretty, to ease the pain, warn others.
The long straight highway going no place for miles
seems designed to claim lives, exact its toll
across a landscape of boulders piled like wishes,
red clay-bottomed washes, parched creek beds
which must return to life in cruel flash floods.
We drink to kill the pain, begetting more,
drink to fit in and find ourselves forced out.
My brother, the man outside Taos Pueblo said in thanks,
Thank you, my brother, and the blood bond may have
been deep.
Perhaps he too survived to everyone's surprise
the alcoholic world with few escape routes,
avoiding suicide, prison time,
being memorialized on a small white cross.
It's a happy thought anyway in a land, harsh and bleak,
where feathered survivors have supernatural powers
and may someday compel the dead to speak.

Lenses
Isbella Diaz

An eye for an eye
Is this what we call justice?
Makes the whole world blind

The Yard
Khalid Karim

Walking the yard is like a never-ending journey,
one filled with reminiscing and yearning
sadness and hurting.

But you keep on walking and spending time alone
pondering your past, wishing you were home,
hating your mistakes and wanting to atone.

And though remembering what you've lost will be painful
it is a hurt that you should learn from,
so face it and be grateful.

You'll walk and find yourself wanting to shed tears
but you won't because of your peers
and their opinions of you heightens your fears.

But they're thinking and feeling the same thing,
still no one is honest with themselves
and that's a strange thing, so how do we change things?

And you walk on looking at fences, fences, and more
fences,
while the cold attitudes and concrete
heightens some and numbs other senses.

The conversations you hear is ignorance spilling out the
mouths of fools,
so silly they'd cause your ears to bleed,
childish men whose lives went unschooled.

The birds above mock your confinement
but you will walk on, often alone

while the clowns around you, mock your refinement.

But you keep putting one foot in front of the other
patiently persevering, moving closer to your
sister, mom, father, son, aunt or brother.

You endure because you must
because to do otherwise
is to abandon faith and that betrays His trust.

So you keep walking this never-ending journey
because there's always a glimmer of hope
that you will fulfill your yearning.

About the Editors and Contributors

MARISA FEIN (Editor-in-Chief) is thrilled to serve as the 2016 Tacenda Literary Magazine Editor and would like to thank everyone who has made this issue possible, especially Professor Johnson. As an undergraduate student at American University pursuing a degree in literature and gender studies, Marisa has developed a passion for social justice, particularly within the context of gender equality. She has previously worked to further women's empowerment by leading community education events and interning with the DC branch of the National Organization for Women. Through her work at BleakHouse Publishing, she has furthered her interest in prison reform and has become an advocate for social justice.

ROBERT JOHNSON (Consulting Editor) is a Professor of Justice, Law and Criminology at American University, Editor and Publisher of BleakHouse Publishing, and a widely published and award winning author of books and articles on crime and punishment, including works of social science, law, and fiction. He has testified or testified expert affidavits on capital and other criminal cases in many venues, including US state and federal courts, the U.S. Congress, and the European Commission of Human Rights. He is best known for his book, *Death Work: A Study of the Modern Execution Process*, which won the Outstanding Book Award of the Academy of Criminal Justice Sciences. Johnson is a Distinguished Alumnus of the Nelson A. Rockefeller College of Public Affairs and Policy, University at Albany, State University of New York.

ANTWON is a 26-year-old member of Free Minds Book Club & Writing Workshop, currently incarcerated in federal prison. Antwon's poetry has previously appeared in the Free Minds publications *The Untold Story of the Real Me* and *They Call Me 299-359*. Antwon loves to read books about African-American history

CIERA BURCH is a senior at American University in Washington, D.C. majoring in Literature and History. She hopes to use her passion for writing and storytelling to make sure that diversity and representation are more than hashtags.

CURTIS is a 23-year-old member of Free Minds Book Club & Writing Workshop, currently incarcerated in federal prison. Curtis's poetry has previously appeared in the Free Minds publications *The Untold Story of the Real Me* and *They Call Me 299-359*. Curtis is studying African-American Literature while incarcerated, and one of his goals is to travel across the country.

D'ANGELO is a 21-year-old member of Free Minds Book Club & Writing Workshop, currently incarcerated in federal prison. D'Angelo's poetry has previously appeared in the 2015 issue of *Tacenda* and Free Minds publication *The Untold Story of the Real Me*. D'Angelo dreams of owning his own business.

ISBELLA DIAZ is currently the program manager at the National Press Foundation, a non-profit in D.C. that works to make good journalists better. Prior to joining NPF, Isbella worked as programming assistant of news for Washington's WMAL 630 radio station, reporting and writing on both international and local Washington issues. Isbella also worked for both the digital media and talk show teams at CCTV America. She helped maintain the channel's social media accounts, website and online broadcasts. Isbella graduated from American University with a MA in International Media in 2015 and a BA in Broadcast Journalism in 2013.

DIMITRI is a 24-year-old member of Free Minds Book Club & Writing Workshop, currently incarcerated in Maryland. Dimitri's poetry has previously appeared in the Free Minds publication *They Call Me 299-359*. Dimitri wants to go to college and become a personal trainer.

MAUREEN GERAGHTY has been teaching in alternative school settings for 25 years. She and her two school-aged children live in Portland, Oregon. She self-published a book of poetry entitled, *Look Up- Poems of a Life* and has poetry published in *ReThinking Schools*, mamazine.com, mothering.com and *Teaching with Heart*. Her essay, "Our Better Angels," will appear in the anthology *Stand There Shining*. She and Jevon published an article, "Writing Outside the Bars" with the National Writing Project's journal, *The Quarterly*, which is a portion of a book they are currently working on, entitled *Between Writers and Lifers*.

ANNA HASSANYEH studied Law at the University of Westminster and worked for the Crown Prosecution Service in London, England. She has also worked as a teacher. Anna's published short stories include "The Discarded Ragdoll" and "Daisy Train," both published in *Writers' Forum* (a UK Literary Magazine), and "Demons and Lollipops," published on Litro Online. Still living in London, Anna now runs a computer security company with her husband and spends most of her free time reading and writing.

JOANNA HEANEY, an alumna of the American University class of 2015, uses poetry to express her reactions to illogical workings of the criminal justice system. Originally from Rhode Island, Heaney was drawn to Washington, DC for its vibrant political climate. Heaney now works in food & hospitality PR in Washington, although she continues looking for chances to further her understanding of the concept of justice.

KIMBERLY HRICKO has been incarcerated in the Maryland Correctional Institution for Women since 1998. Kimberly is an active member of her prison environment, often pushing the administration for positive change. She has worked as an AutoCAD Space Planner/Designer for the Maryland Correctional Enterprises since 2006. She lives with her rescue cat (Friends of Anne Arundel County Animal Center's Prison Rescue Cat Association www.faacac.org) on the Merit Pod, a housing unit for those with excellent institutional records. She was able to start a Book Club with the help of Judge Brenda Murray (American Association of Women Judges). The club is quite successful, about to begin its twentieth session and tenth year. The Book Club eventually spawned a Writing Seminar facilitated by Peter Carlson, author and former Washington Post Columnist. Prisons in Iowa and California have been inspired by MCIW to start their own Book Club. Kimberly is also very involved in MCIW's Building Bridges Project, a victim outreach program focused on accountability, responsibility and forgiveness. She finds purpose and comfort in speaking to victim's groups, hoping to help them begin to heal through honest dialogue. She is serving a life sentence with parole and supports legislation that will reverse the Maryland's "life means life" policy under which no parole eligible lifer has been released since 1995

I.S. is a 20-year-old member of Free Minds Book Club & Writing Workshop, currently incarcerated in federal prison. His poetry has previously appeared in the Free Minds publication *The Untold Story of the Real Me.* His goal is to be a chef.

JEVON JACKSON has published two books of poetry entitled *Why the Prisoner Only Writes Love Poems* and *Handwritten Poems* online with PrisonsFoundation.org. His poems also appear in the publications *J Journal* and *The Oyez Review.* Jevon is an ambassador and correspondent for *The Community News,* a publication out of Milwaukee, Wisconsin. He is co-author of the in-progress book, *Between Writers and Lifers.* Jevon currently resides in the New Lisbon Correctional Institution in Wisconsin.

KHALID KARIM was born and raised in Washington, DC and, though life was very far from pleasant, will always recognize the love and efforts of his family in their work to do what they could for his large family whom he cherishes and supports. Karim has been locked up for 23 years for crimes committed when he was young but he has used this time wisely by receiving his GED and also becoming HVAC and OSHA certified, in addition to also completing a number of other self-help programs. He has also been heavily involved in various mentoring programs and has put together and facilitated a number of educational and entertainment programs involving plays, spoken word, rap, and positive speeches. He is currently working on a poetry book and a book that shares his prison experience. He has used his time in prison to study his mistakes and to improve himself and any and all who will listen. He truly wants to give back by helping others learn who they're actually intended to be so that they can do and be better.

JOSEF KREBS has a chapbook published by Etched Press and his poetry also appears in *Agenda, the Bicycle Review, Calliope, Mouse Tales Press, The Corner Club Press, The FictionWeek Literary Review, Burningword Literary Journal, The Aurorean, Inscape, Crack the Spine, The Cape Rock, Carcinogenic Poetry, The Bangalore Review,* and *The Cats Meow.* A short story has been published in *blazeVOX*. He's written three novels and five screenplays. His film was successfully screened at Santa Cruz and Short Film Corner of Cannes film festival.

RICK LYON'S book of poems *Bell 8* was published by BOA Editions. His work has appeared in *The Missouri Review, The Nation* and *The New Republic.* He's a boat captain and also an RV transporter making deliveries throughout the U.S. and Canada. A longtime resident of Essex, Connecticut, he now lives with his wife Lisa LeVally on a horse farm in Des Plaines, Illinois

EMILY PAULSRUD is a political science student at Sciences Po in Paris, France. She studies why political actors act the way do, but is also interested in how institutional systems affect the people who live in them, including the criminal justice system.

RAFAEL is a 22-year-old member of Free Minds Book Club & Writing Workshop, currently incarcerated in federal prison. Rafael's poetry has previously appeared in the Free Minds publication *The Untold Story of the Real Me*. Rafael's goal is to graduate from college.

ALFRED "SPOKEN TRUTH" is a 37-year-old member of Free Minds Book Club & Writing Workshop, currently serving a 24-year sentence in the state of Virginia. Alfred writes under the pen name "Spoken Truth." His poetry has previously appeared in the 2015 issue of *Tacenda*, and his poem "Crocus" won the Best Poem Award.

VINCENT is a 26-year-old member of Free Minds Book Club & Writing Workshop, currently incarcerated in federal prison. Vincent's poetry has previously appeared in the Free Minds publication *The Untold Story of the Real Me*. Vincent loves to read plays and biographies.

www.ingramcontent.com/pod-product-compliance
Lightning Source LLC
Chambersburg PA
CBHW070317120726
47910CB00007B/2521

* 9 7 8 0 9 9 9 6 1 1 6 2 2 0 *